Mysterious

RoseDog Books
585 Alpha Drive, Suite 103
Pittsburgh, PA 15238
Visit our website at *www.rosedogbookstore.com*

ISBN: 978-1-6461-0251-8
eISBN: 978-1-6461-0893-0

Mysterious

Kayla McIntosh

PITTSBURGH, PENNSYLVANIA 15238

Episode 1

One day there were three sisters living in a penthouse. Their names were Ruby, Dorothy, and Bella. One night while they were sleeping something sneaked in. They looked like robots. Their names were Freddy, Bonnie, Chica, and Foxy. "Guys, I don't think I can sleep" said Ruby. "Why? By the way I need to sleep. I have cheerleading practice tomorrow", said Dorothy. "I know, but something feels weird like somebody's in the penthouse", said Ruby. "That's ridiculous. Didn't Mom and Dad lock up the place when they went out for dinner?" said Bella. "Can everybody stop yapping and go to sleep!" said Dorothy. "Guys can we please go downstairs?" said Ruby. "Fine!" said Dorothy. The girls went downstairs. "Dorothy are those robots?" said Bella.

Episode 2

"We need to get back upstairs now", said Dorothy. "Wait a minute, who are they", said Ruby. The girls ran upstairs and hid. "What do we do? We can't stay upstairs forever!", said Bella. "I know but mom and dad said if there is an intruder, call them" said Dorothy. "It's not really an intruder, they are robots" said Ruby. "It is an intruder, if they are in the penthouse it makes them intruders" said Dorothy. "Stop fighting! Nobody has time for this" says Bella. "Your right" said Ruby. "Wait a minute, I found a large book and it looks like, just like the robot's downstairs!" said Dorothy. "What do you mean?", said Ruby. "Do you think Mom and Dad left that clue for us", said Bella. "Hmmm, I am not sure! But we need to find out who they are, "said Dorothy.

Episode 3

"Ok so what do we do? Do we fight?" said Ruby. "Ruby are dumb" said Bella. "Those monsters look like they want to steal our souls" said Bella. "Well she isn't wrong" said Dorothy. "Wait I have an idea, lets just squirt them with water", said Ruby. "Well forget that plan, what about the book", said Bella. The girls looked in the book. "They are not called robots, they are called animatronics", said Dorothy. "Ummm, nobody knows what that means?" said Bella and Ruby. "It's says they are dangerous", said Dorothy. "Umm guys I hear something, I think they are coming up stairs", said Bella. The girls hid under the bed. "Oh my God I am so scared", said Ruby. "They heard us, let's run" said Dorothy. So, the girls went to the pizzeria. "What are we doing at the pizzeria?", said Bella.

Episode 4

"I am looking in the book, and this is where the animatronics were formed," said Dorothy. "So were in deep craziness", said Ruby. "Pretty much", said Bella. "You know Bella, this is all your fault!", said Ruby. "Wait a minute, how is this my fault", said Bella. "Because you screamed and ruined our hiding spot", said Ruby. "Omg! Stop fighting. We are in deep trouble", said Dorothy. "Who cares!" says Ruby. "Ok lets just squirt the animatronics with water", said Bella. "We can't squirt them with water. They are immune to it. If we squirted them, they won't be on the floor for long," said Dorothy. "Ohh no! I think they are here," said Ruby. The girls ran in the office. "This office is full of camera's, we can spy on the animatronics!", said Dorothy.

Épisode 5

"Hello", said Kamora. "Hello", said Dorothy. "Do you guys need help?", said Shariyah. "Wait, who are you?" said Ruby. "My name is Kamora, and this is my friend Shariyah", said Kamora. "Wait what are you guys doing here?" said Shariyah. "Running from monster robots, hello!" said Bella. "They are not called robots", said Dorothy. "Wait are you guys running from the animatronics", said Shariyah. "The book says, this guy named purple guy isn't a good person at all," said Dorothy. "So, you don't have any good news", said Bella. "How could we have good news if creepy robots follow us everywhere," said Ruby. "Can everybody calm down," said Shariyah. "They are banging down the door" said Ruby. "Wait, where is Bella", said Kamora. "They took her!" said Shariyah.

Episode 6—Find Bella

"Wait where is Demorion," said Kamora. "Who is Demorion," asked Dorothy. "He's a friend from old orchard, he might still be in the lock room," said Shariyah. "People our sister got taken away by some crazy robot," said Ruby. "We need to get her back," said Ruby. "But, how can we find her she can be anywhere," said Dorothy. "True but maybe not anywhere mayne she is at a room that only the purple guy knows," said Kamora. "Kamora we don't know who purple guy is, and we don't know what he looks like," said Shariyah. "Guys are we still on the topic of our missing sister? She's been gone for an hour," said Ruby. "We should not go out there because they can take us like they took Bella." "Let's just find her and hope she is okay," said Shariyah.

Episode 7—Find Bella and Demorion

The girls sneaked out the hallway and went to find Demorion and Bella. Demorion said, "Kamora?" Kamora said, "Demorion?" "Demorion are you alright?" asked Shariyah. "Yeah," said Demorion. "Ok we found Demorion, we need to find Bella," said Dorothy. "Guys I found Bella, she is in the locked room," said Ruby. "Yeah, but its locked we don't have a key," said Demorion. "I have a hair clip, I think I can pick the lock," said Ruby. "I almost got it." Dorothy and Ruby you guys saved me," said Bella. "Who are they?" Bella asked. "Their names are Kamora, Shariyah, and Demorion." "Ok, well my name is Bella!"

Episode 8—We need to get out of here

"Umm guys we have a problem," said Bella. "What now," said Ruby. "The doors are locked we can't get out of the pizzeria," said Bella. "What do you mean we can't be locked in, its impossible. I didn't lock the door," said Dorothy. "Guys maybe Dorothy didn't lock the door, maybe purple guy did so we couldn't escape," said Kamora. "Kamora, don't you think that he locked the door because he is the owner of the pizzeria?" asked Shariyah. "Shariyah is right, wait a minute don't you still have your hair clip," said Dorothy. "Yeah, but this door is jammed good."

Episode 9—Let us Out

"Guys we have another problem," said Ruby. "What's the problem?" asked Demorion. "I lost the hair clip," said Ruby. "You lost the hair clip, why did you lose it?" asked Dorothy. "I didn't think we would need it anymore," said Ruby. "That doesn't mean you should just throw it away," said Dorothy. "Dorothy, nobody knew we were going to be locked in the pizzeria," said Demorion. "Guys calm down nobody getting out," said Bella. "May I remind you that we are still here with animatronics," said Dorothy. "Stop arguing, we don't have time for this," said Demorion. "Guys be quiet we need to make a run for it," said Bella. "But, where? There is no where to go," said Dorothy. "RUN!" said Demorion. So, they ran and ran.

Episode 10—Just remembered

As they were running Demorion just realized that he forgot his friends Jay'lena, Kamora, and Shariyah. "Hold up!" said Demorion. "What?" said Dorothy. "Where's Kamora, Shariyah, and Jay'lena," asked Demorion. "I don't know," said Ruby. "Let's check the security camera's" said Dorothy. They checked the cameras. "Oh No!" said Dorothy. "The animatronics took Jay'lena!" said Ruby. "Why didn't they take Shariyah or Kamora," asked Demorion. "I don't know," said Dorothy. "But we need to find them!" said Demorion. They ran to Kamora and Shariyah. "Shariyah," Kamora"..yelled Dorothy. "What?" said Kamora. "What happened?" said Demorion. "The stupid robots left us on the ground," said Kamora. "Why did they take Jay'lena," asked Dorothy. "I don't know but maybe they need her for research," said Sydney. "What? Who's that?"

Episode 11—New Girl

"Wait who are you and get out of the shadows," said Demorion. The mysterious girl came out of the shadows. "Hello," said new girl. "Wait what's your name," asked Bella. "My name is Sydney," said the new girl. "Ok nice to meet you Sydney, I guess" said Ruby. "Wait, let's talk somewhere else, I don't want to get caught out in the open" said Dorothy. They ran back into the office. "Ok so explain why you're here in the pizzeria?" said Bella. "Ok so my sister Leah dared me to go in the pizzeria for 24 hours," said Sydney. "And, I said yes to it because I love the pizzeria!" she said. "Anyway, I am looking for a big book," said Sydney. "You mean the book that is on the floor right now?" said Dorothy. "Yes, it has a lot of information about purple guy," said Sydney.

Episode 12—Information ahead

The kids looked in the book. "It says purple guys plan is to have a animatronic army to take over the world for all eternity," said Dorothy. "For once why can't we have good news," said Ruby. "Since when have we had good news everything right now is pure bad news," said Dorothy. "Guys calm down, all we have to do is stop his plan," said Sydney. "So how can we do that without him noticing," said Kamora. "We just have to keep a low profile," said Shariyah. "Ok," said Ruby. The kids looked at the security camera trying to find Jay'lena and where they took her but all they saw was purple guards guarding a room that maybe Jay'lena might be in. "Guys I think I found Jay'lena but not in a good way."

Episode 13 — We need Jay'lena

"Guys I found Jay'lena, but we need to armor up," said Sydney. "Ok well I found a bat," said Dorothy. "And, I found a hammer," said Kamora. "So, everybody has something to wack with," said Sydney. "Yea," said Kamora. "Ok," said Sydney. The kids ran to look for Jay'lena but as soon as they got there they were surrounded by fear. "Guys I am scared," said Ruby. "Guys all we have to do is whack some heads," said Sydney. The kids started to fight the guards and luckily they beat some so they were able to sneak in. "Jay'lena," said Sydney. "Yes," said Jay'lena. "Are you ok," said Dorothy. "I don't think so I have a wire in my arm, and it keeps shocking me!" said Jay'lena. "Don't worry we will get it out of you," said Demorion. After several minutes they finally got it out of her.

Episode 14—Dizzy Troubles

"I feel dizzy," said Jay'lena. "Ok all we have to do is sneak by the guard again," said Sydney. "But then we have to wack some heads again," said Demorion. "Who cares at least we saved Jay'lena," said Bella. "Ok let's wack some heads and remember to becareful with Jay'lena." The kids fought the guards, but the guards were more vicious. "Oh my gosh I can't believe we did that," said Shariyah. "That was interesting and kind of fun," said Kamora. "I know right," said Sydney. "Anyway, why did they put wires in your arm," asked Bella. "They said they need information on me," said Jay'lena. "Wait, what do they need information on you for," said Dorothy. "I don't know," said Jay'lena. "Guys I just remembered any kid purple guy takes, they go missing," said Sydney. "Well that's not good," said Shariyah.

Episode 15—Missing Girl

"She can't go missing Sydney," said Dorothy. "Yes, she can purple guy is a horrible person and he always gets what he wants," said Sydney. "But why Jay'lena she didn't do anything," said Ruby. "It doesn't matter he is crazy," said Sydney. "Maybe we are in his way maybe he wants us gone," said Kamora. "We don't know, maybe she will be ok," said Shariyah. "Shariyah, Sydney just said purple guy always gets what he wants," said Kamora. "I know but we can keep her safe," said Shariyah. "But then he will come for us as well," said Ruby. "Guys your scaring me," said Jay'lena. "Sorry Jay'lena but Shariyah keeps starting an argument," said Kamora. "I am not starting no argument Kamora," said Shariyah. "Yes, you are," said Kamora. "You know what Kamora, I am leaving," said Shariyah. "You can't leave the doors are locked," said Dorothy. "Whatever," said Shariyah.

Episode 16—Old girl verses new girl

"Wow that was unexpected," said Ruby. "Wait why did they fight," said Bella. "Because Shariyah and Kamora are fighting over Jay'lena's choices," said Dorothy. "Well my choice is to make Jay'lena be safe, not putting our lives on the line." "Guy don't you hear that cracking noise," said Dorothy. "Well now I hear it, yeah" said Jay'lena. There was a large sack on the floor. Its been there for a while but the girls didn't mind until now. "Should we open it," said Kamora. "Maybe yes, maybe no," said Bella. They opened the sack and..." Natalya!" said everybody. "Umm..Hi, guys" said Natalya. "Natalya what are you doing here," asked Kamora. "Anyway, guys I just want to say sorr...." "Excuse me who's that?" said Shariyah. "Its Natalya joining the group," said Kamora. "You can't replace me Kamora," said Shariyah. "Well don't turn you back on the group," said Kamora.

Episode 17 — Haters

"Kamora protecting her is the best choice that we have," said Shariyah. "So, we are putting our lives on the line," Kamora said. "I am not saying that, I am saying protecting her from danger," said Shariyah. "Stop it! This has been going on quite enough," said Dorothy. "Yeah we are all in danger anyways," said Ruby. "It's not your decision guys, its Jay'lena decision," said Bella. "Your right," said Kamora. "Anyways sorry about that, I'm Shariyah. What's your name?" said Shariyah. "Umm I am Natalya!" "Nice to meet you," said Shariyah. "Anyway, can we focus on us for a second," said Dorothy. "Right we need to be careful of what we're facing right now," said Kamora. "Ok if Jay'lena is in danger we need to act fast and quickly," said Bella. "True true. But we need to be smart about it," said Sydney.

Episode 18—Trap Purple Guy!

"Guys I have an idea," said Sydney. "What is it," said Natalya. "Let's trap purple guy," said Sydney. "So that's your idea," said Natalya. "Sydney do you know how much danger that is," said Shariyah. "I know but this is our only hope to escape," said Sydney. "Okay what do you need," said Kamora. "Okay I need rope, string, thread, and a net," said Sydney. "And where are you going to find that," said Dorothy. "In purple guys office," said Sydney. "WHAT?" said Ruby. "I am not going in there," said Bella. "Guys this is only hope," said Sydney. "Fine fine," said Kamora. "Wait let's check the cameras," said Ruby. "Guys purple guy is gone he is not in his office," said Dorothy. "That's good we have a better advantage," said Sydney. The kids ran to the office. "Ok this is all we need," said Sydney. "Let's get grabbing," said Kamora.

Episode 19 — Waiting for the prey

"There's no rope," said Shariyah. "What do you mean there is no rope," said Sydney. "I mean its not in here," said Shariyah. "Ok that means we need to find rope somewhere else," said Kamora. "Guys I found the rope," said Sydney. The kids ran back to where they came from and started setting up the trap. "Guys I also found a note in his office, "..

Note reads: Dear Bollon Boy, it's our time to take over the world for all eternity, but we need to get rid of these girls—Father. "Why does he have a note," said Sydney. "Let's focus on the trap first," said Bella.

Episode 20—We did it We escaped

"Ok the trap is set we just have to wait," said Dorothy. "Ok but what time is it," said Kamora. "Its 5 o'clock we just have one more hour to escape from this horrible place," said Natalya. "Ok guys purple guy is here," said Ruby. Purple guy approached the door. "Omgosh we got him," said Ruby. The kids ran and ran. "Guys there is a maze to the door," said Dorothy. "This just keeps getting worse and worse," said Jay'lena. "Omgosh when will this end," said Shariyah. The kids ran through each maze but couldn't find the door. "Guys I see an exit sign," said Jay'lena. The kids ran and made it outside. "Wait did we make it," said Kamora. "We did it!" said Dorothy. The kids ran to their homes. Their parents were worried and wondered where they were. "Woohoo!" said Sydney.

SEASON 2

Episode 1—Sleepover

"Guy's lets have a sleep over tonight," said Sydney. "Why," said Bella. "For fun," said Sydney. "Ok but my mom said to play nice," said Dorothy. (The doorbell rings) "Guy's Sydney is here," said Ruby. "That was fast," said Bella. Sydney went upstairs to the girl's bedroom. "Guy's remember when we were at the pizzeria," said Dorothy. "Yeah about that, Dad is taking us back to the pizzeria," said Ruby. "WHAT!" said all the girls. "Were not going to no pizzeria," said Bella. "Wait did you guys tell your parents about the incident," said Sydney. "No, we didn't want them to worry," "Well they should worry now," said Sydney. "Does your brother Nakai know," said Sydney. "Since when do we tell our brother anything," said Dorothy. "Anyways where is Shariyah and Kamora," said Dorothy. "They are out of town with their families," said Ruby. "Ok guys let go to bed, I am very tired," said Bella. The girls went to sleep and agreed to talk about it in the morning.

Episode 2—We need to gear up

"**G**uy's wake up! It's morning," said Nakai. "Nakai why do you always wake us up all the time," said Dorothy. "Number 1 because it is fun, number 2 because Mom is taking us to the pizzeria," said Nakai. "Wait can we take Sydney with us," said Bella. "Yeah whatever," said Nakai. "Okay we need to find the book," said Dorothy. "What book," said Ruby. "The book we found a couple days back," said Dorothy. "Oh, right it's somewhere under the bed," said Sydney. The looked under the bed. "I found it," said Sydney. "Ok we should bring it with us," said Bella. "Someone needs to take it," said Bella. "And I think it should be Dorothy," said Bella. "Wait why me," said Dorothy. "Because I left my backpack at Grandpa's house," said Bella. "And, you're the only one who has a backpack," said Ruby. "Fine," said Dorothy. The girls showered and got dressed. "Hey Nakai," said Bella. "What?" said Nakai. "Can you tell Mom to cancel," said Ruby. "Fine but your doing my chores," said Nakai. "Deal," said Bella.

Episode 3—Are time has come

"Guys I bought us some time," said Bella. "And how did you do that," said Dorothy. "By doing his chores," said Bella. "Ok well why you do that, I have a perfect idea," said Dorothy. "And that is," said Ruby. "Get rid of Nakai," said Dorothy. "And why should we do that," said Bella. "Well Nakai will automatically know something is up if we keep putting it off," said Dorothy. "Dorothy I was not asking for that part, my question is why should we get rid of him," said Bella. "Well do you want to put Nakai in danger," said Dorothy. "Well aren't we putting ourselves in danger too," said Bella. "It doesn't matter we would do anything to save our parents and the whole community," said Dorothy. "And since when did the community do anything for us," said Ruby. "The community doesn't need to do anything," said Dorothy. "Okay I am done with this conversation. I am going to bed," said Bella.

Episode 4—Midnight Adventures

"**G**uy's wake up," said Dorothy. "UGH," said Bella "Fine I'm up" said Bella. "Okay then wake up Ruby, it's really important," said Dorothy. "And what is so important to wake us up in the middle of the night," said Bella. "JUST WAKE UP RUBY," yelled Dorothy. "Ok, geez!" said Bella. "Ruby wake up Dorothy wants to show us something," said Bella. "I hate you Dorothy," said Ruby. "You can hate me all you want, but there is something unusual I need to show you," said Dorothy. Dorothy leads her sisters to their parents' room. "Wait where is mom and dad," said Bella. "I don't know," said Dorothy. "I woke up in the middle of the night to get milk. I didn't hear any snoring from Mom and Dad, so I went to the doorway and still didn't hear it, and turned on the light and they were gone," said Dorothy. "That doesn't make sense they can't disappear out of thin air Dorothy," said Bella. "Wait what if the robots followed us home," said Ruby. "That's a good theory but we don't know that for sure," said Bella.

Episode 5—Missing parents

The kids went back to their room. "I can't believe they are gone and so is Nakai," said Bella. "Wait what if we look on the security cameras to see what took them," said Dorothy. The kids looked at the security cameras and couldn't believe what they saw. "Oh my gosh my theory was right," said Ruby. "They got taken away by FNaf robots," said Bella. "Wow that was unexpected," said Dorothy. "No kidding," said Bella. "Looks like purple guy wasn't finished with us yet," said Ruby. "He must have a reason to steal our parents and brother," said Dorothy. "Unless he wants to get us back for doing the trap to him when we tried to escape," said Bella. "But that doesn't mean anything," said Dorothy. "Maybe that meant something to him but never mind that now we got better things to worry about now," said Ruby. "All we need to do is go back to the pizzeria and maybe we could make a deal with purple guy," said Dorothy.

Episode 6—Gear up this is a great plan

"Dorothy your ideas are always great but this one is not so good," said Bella. "I have to agree," said Ruby. "Guys this is the only way we can save mom, dad, and nakai," Said Dorothy. "She may be right," said Ruby. "But its still not a good idea," said Bella. "Well do you have any better ideas," said Ruby. "Ummm.. exactly now let's go with your idea Dorothy," said Ruby. "Ok here's the plan we sneak into the pizzeria quietly without anyone seeing us and go to the camera room and disconnect the camera's so they can't trace us back," said Dorothy. "I'll admit this is a really good idea," said Bella. "I know that's right," said Ruby. "Ok since we all agree about my idea than let's gear up," said Dorothy. The girls looked in their drawers for clothes. Dorothy wore a black and white shirt with a leather jacket, black jeans, with lace up boots. Bella wore light blue shirt with dark pants and lace up boots.

Episode 7—Sneaking In

"Everyone dressed," asked Dorothy. "Yep," said Ruby and Bella. "Ok let's leave the penthouse because the door man Tony should be asleep by now," said Dorothy. The girls went down the elevator to the lobby and snuck out the door into the dark alley. "There is mom and dad's car maybe we can drive it," said Ruby. (Sighs) "We're going to die at the pizzeria, but you want us to die now," said Dorothy. "The animatronics live in the shadows they could be watching us right now," said Ruby. "Well we do need better transportation," said Bella." "Fine but if we die it will be all on you two," said Dorothy. The girls got in the car. Dorothy agreed to take the steering wheel. "Um guys how do we slow down," said Dorothy. "Why do you want to know," said Bella. "Because the limit we are going is 100SPEED!" said Dorothy. "You don't know how to drive Dorothy," said Ruby. "Well sorry I didn't take my driver's license test" said Dorothy. "We're going to DIE," said Ruby.

Episode 8—Police Involved

"What do I do I don't know how to drive," said Dorothy. "Oh, great the police just our luck," said Ruby. "Come on man this is your fault Bella," said Dorothy. "Dorothy in a time like this it isn't time to be throwing shade around and this isn't my fault it's Ruby," said Bella. "And how is this my fault," said Ruby. "You're the one who talked us into driving this car," said Bella. "You said we needed better transportation," said Ruby. "Yes, but I didn't mean a car!" said Bella. "Police pull over the car, I repeat pull over!" Police cars surrounding every part of the car. "Omgosh!" said Dorothy. "I am sorry guys I didn't mean to put us in the situation," said Ruby. "We win together, we fail together that's how it always has been," said Dorothy. "Wait I have an idea what if we close down fready fasbear," said Dorothy. "And how are we going to do that," said Bella. Before Dorothy could say what, she was going to say, "guys there's a newspaper down here and it's about Fready Fasbear," said Ruby.

Episode 9—Surrender

"Why does mom and dad have a newspaper about Fready Fasbear Pizzeria," said Dorothy. "Surrender or prepare for the worst," yelled the Police. "We're running out of time," said Dorothy. The kids came out of the car with their hands up. "Finally, wait…your little kids in car," Police stated. "Police lots of things have been happening to us," said Dorothy. "Like what?" said Police "Have you ever heard of Fready's Fasbear Pizzeria?" asked Ruby. "We can't talk about them in the open. We need to take them to the police station and find out what they know and see what they know about the missing children," said the Police. The girls went into the car without saying anything. They got to the police station, they went in and sat down. "I can't believe we are in a police station," said Ruby. "If mom and dad were here, we would be grounded for life," said Dorothy. "No kidding," said Bella. "We need to talk," said the Police.

Episode 10—They want you

"**O**kay!" said Dorothy. "Your in trouble the only reason why they took your parents is to lure you into a trap," said the Police. "What trap," said Dorothy. "These monsters want you, they want your soul," said the Police. "But why our souls," said Ruby. "Purple guy has this plan to make an animatronic army. He thinks kids are to rude and disrespectful and deserved to be punished," said the Police. "But we need our parents back," said Bella. "Unless we trick him, but I have a plan, we are going to need a lot of requirements if we want to pull this off. Police may we be excused?" said Dorothy. The girls left the station and walked home when they reached home, they found a note in the bushes.

Note reads:

Aw! Going home so soon. Remember the clock is ticking!

Signed: Purple Guy

CPSIA information can be obtained
at www.ICGtesting.com
Printed in the USA
BVHW040824120320
574403BV00013B/52